To Peter Gibbs,
with thanks

A BRUBAKER, FORD & FRIENDS BOOK,
an imprint of The Templar Company Limited

First published in the UK in hardback in 2011 by Templar Publishing
This softback edition published in 2013 by Templar Publishing,
Deepdene Lodge, Deepdene Avenue, Dorking, Surrey, RH5 4AT, UK
www.templarco.co.uk

1 3 5 7 9 10 8 6 4 2

ISBN 978-1-84877-879-5

Printed in China

Little Bee

Edward Gibbs

B|F|&|F

BRUBAKER, FORD & FRIENDS

AN IMPRINT OF THE TEMPLAR COMPANY LIMITED

Little bee, little bee

why do you flee?

Because there's a
hungry **frog** chasing me!

Hungry frog, hungry frog

why do you flee?

Because there's a
scary **snake** chasing me!

Scary snake, scary snake

why do you flee?

Because there's a mean **mongoose** chasing me!

Mean mongoose, mean mongoose

why do you flee?

Because there's a
hairy **hyena** chasing me!

Hairy hyena, hairy hyena

why do you flee?

Because there's a fierce **lion** chasing me!

Fierce lion, fierce lion

why do you flee?

Because there's a
big **hunter** chasing me!

Because...